Noddy's Great Discovery

HarperCollins *Children's Books*

It was a bustling day in Toyland and the train was just about to pull out of Toy Town Station.

"All aboard!" cried the conductor. "All aboard the Toyland Express!"

Noddy had been watching the trains pull in and out of the station all morning.

"I wish I could do that!" he thought.

As the train started to move, Noddy ran alongside it, waving to all the passengers.

"Choo choo! Choo choo!" cried Noddy, happily.

When the train disappeared into the distance,
Noddy waved goodbye and went to find his friends.

On his way to the square, he noticed something
shining on the ground and bent down to pick it up.

"A gold coin!" Noddy cried, holding it up to the
sun. "This must be my lucky day!"

"What shall I do with it?" thought Noddy. "Maybe I should save it. Or maybe I should buy some delicious sweets with it!"

While Noddy was deciding what to do, he noticed another object sparkling on the ground.

"Another coin!" cried Noddy as he ran over to it. "That makes two! I'll save one coin and buy some sweets with the other."

Noddy was about to set off to buy some sweets when he noticed a third shiny coin on the floor.

"A third coin!" cried Noddy, puzzled.

"What should I do? Should I save two and spend one? Or spend three and save none?"

Before Noddy had time to make a decision, he saw another gold coin on the floor. And then another, and another, and another until he had ten gold coins!

"Wow! That's nearly a fortune! And it's all mine!" Noddy gasped, as he looked down at his coins. "What shall I spend it on?"

Just then, Noddy heard the faint chug-chug of the train in the distance and smiled. He knew exactly what he wanted to do with his money.

Dinah Doll was arranging her new toys on her stall when Noddy came bounding over.

"Dinah Doll! Dinah Doll! I'm going to buy it!" Noddy cried, shaking his golden coins.

"Buy what, Noddy?" asked Dinah Doll, puzzled.

"That brilliant train set!" Noddy cried, excitedly. "Can I buy it? Please?"

"Which set are you talking about?" asked Dinah Doll, laughing at Noddy's excitement.

"You know the one! The one I love!" said Noddy. "The one that looks exactly like the Toyland Express. One engine, three passenger cars and a caboose!"

"I don't remember having anything here like that," Dinah Doll smiled.

"Stop joking with me, Dinah! You know the set I mean," cried Noddy, looking at the stall for his beloved train set.

"I most certainly do, Noddy," chuckled Dinah Doll. "I have to drag that train set out once a week so you can stare at it."

Dinah Doll reached below her stall and pulled out a green and yellow box.

"That's the one!" cried Noddy when he saw the familiar box. "I've wanted it for such a long time but I never had enough money to buy it."

"That's because the set is very expensive, Noddy," said Dinah Doll as she started to put the train set back. "It costs ten gold coins."

Noddy reached into his pocket and proudly displayed his coins.

"Noddy, where did you get that much money?" gasped Dinah Doll. "Did you save it from your taxi driving or did money start falling from the sky?"

"I'm not telling you, but you might be right about the sky part!" Noddy giggled, as Dinah Doll handed him the train set.

When he opened the box, he gasped with delight. "It's more beautiful than I remembered!"

Noddy was so happy he burst into a song.

"It chugga-chugg-chuggas,
And then it goes woo-woo,
And everybody wonders
Where my train is heading to!
It whistles and it rattles,
It clatters down the track,
It travels all around the town
And hurry-scurries back!"

Big-Ears was on his way to see Dinah Doll, when
he saw Noddy playing with the train set.

"That's a very dandy train set you've got
there, Noddy," said Big-Ears.

"I just bought it," Noddy said, happily. "For ten
gold coins."

"Oh, really?" Big-Ears said, slowly. "That's a lot of money. Where did all that money come from?"

"I found the coins on the ground!" Noddy laughed.

Big-Ears frowned. "Someone must have dropped them. Did you tell Mr Plod?"

"Well, no. . ." Noddy began. "Why should I? 'Finders keepers, losers weepers.' That means if I find something, I'm happy and whoever lost it is sad."

"You're right, Noddy. It does make you happy to
find a coin in the ground," Big-Ears replied. "But
you found a LOT of them. Someone probably
needs them and feels very sad indeed."

"But if I tell Mr Plod about the lost coins, the
person who lost them will want them back,"
Noddy said sadly as he glanced at his little train
set. "I'd have to give my train set back!"

"I love my train. I do, I do, I do!" cried Noddy.

Big-Ears patted Noddy on the back. "Noddy, it's up to you to decide what to do."

Noddy looked at his train set on the ground and made his decision. "I'm not going to tell Mr Plod!"

Big-Ears looked disappointed. "Well, if that's what you really want."

Meanwhile, Mr Plod was walking around Toy Town putting up Lost and Found posters. Big-Ears and Noddy went to see if they could help.

"Is something wrong, Mr Plod?" Big-Ears asked, helpfully.

"It's all rather sad," Mr Plod said, frowning. "It seems when Mrs Skittle was out shopping this morning, she had a hole in her purse and all her coins fell out."

"How many coins fell out?" Noddy gulped.

"Ten coins. Can you believe it?" Mr Plod replied. "It would be wonderful if someone found the money. Mrs Skittle has lots of children to feed, and she worked so hard for those coins."

When Noddy realised what had happened, he knew what he had to do. He must give the coins back to poor Mrs Skittle.

He packed his train set into his box and slowly walked back to Dinah Doll's stall.

"Hello, Noddy!" said Dinah Doll. "How is your new train set?"

"It's perfect," said Noddy, quietly. "But I need to ask you a favour."

Noddy explained what had happened and gave the train set back in return for ten gold coins.

Noddy set off to find Mrs Skittle but bumped into Mr Plod along the way.

"Hello, Mr Plod. Would you give this money back to Mrs Skittle?" Noddy said, handing over the ten coins. "I found it on the ground this morning."

"My, my, Noddy. That was a very good and honest thing to do!" Mr Plod said, happily. "Mrs Skittle will be thrilled!"

Big-Ears came to find Noddy when he heard the news from Mr Plod.

"You asked Dinah Doll to take your train set back and return the money," said Big-Ears. "I'm very glad you did the right thing, Noddy. Very glad indeed."

"I suppose so," Noddy said, in agreement. "Sometimes doing the right thing isn't always the most fun thing."

Later that day Noddy was sitting at home
thinking about his little train set, when there was
a knock at the door.

Mrs Skittle had come to thank Noddy.
"I wanted to come over here personally and
thank you for returning my coins. You were very,
VERY kind," Mrs Skittle said, happily.

Then Big-Ears popped his head round the door.
"And honest!" he chimed.

"I'm glad you got your money back,
Mrs Skittle," Noddy said, kindly.

Mrs Skittle looked at Big-Ears and smiled.

"We have a little surprise for you, too," she
said, laughing. "We asked the Toyland train driver
if you could drive the train tomorrow. And he
said yes!"

"Really?! Me?" Noddy said taking a step back in surprise. "Can I blow the whistle, too?"

"Of course you can!" Mrs Skittle laughed.

"To make things even better, this is a reward from all of us for being so good!" said Dinah Doll, as she handed Noddy a box.

Noddy took the box and peeped inside.
"The engine from the train set! Thank you
everybody!" cried Noddy, happily.

"And you can come in and buy the other
parts one at a time until you have bought the
whole set. That is if you want the whole set,"
Dinah Doll joked.

"Of course I want them all!" said Noddy,
laughing. "Finders may not always be keepers but
I'm definitely going to keep this!"

The next day, Noddy raced to Toy Town train station. Big-Ears, Mrs Skittle and Mr Plod had all gathered to watch Noddy's big moment.

"Choo choo!" cried Noddy as he approached the station.

"All aboard the Toyland Express!" shouted the conductor. "Today's driver is Noddy!"

Noddy jumped on board and waved to his friends.

"Hurray for Noddy!" they shouted from the platform.

"Thank you, everybody! This is the best day of my life!" Noddy laughed as he blew the whistle and the train pulled out of Toy Town Station.

First published in Great Britain by HarperCollins Children's Books in 2007
HarperCollins Children's Books is a division of HarperCollins Publishers Ltd,
77-85 Fulham Palace Road, Hammersmith, London W6 8JB

1 3 5 7 9 10 8 6 4 2

ISBN-10: 0-00-722353-6
ISBN-13: 978-0-00-722353-4

Printed and bound by
Printing Express Ltd, Hong Kong

NODDY™

Star in your very own PERSONALISED Noddy book!

In just **3** easy steps your child can join Noddy in a Toyland adventure!

1 Go to www.MyNoddyBook.co.uk

2 Personalise your book

3 Checkout!

3 Great Noddy adventures to choose from:

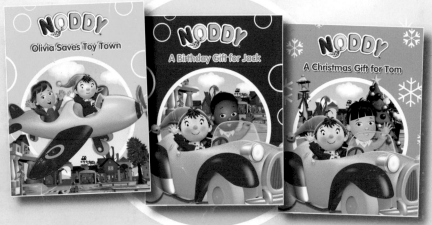

'Your child' Saves Toytown
Soar through a rainbow in Noddy's aeroplane to help him save Toytown.

A Gift for 'your child'
Noddy composes a song for your child in this story for a special occasion.

A Christmas Gift for 'your child'
Noddy composes a song for your child in a Christmas version of the above story.

Visit today to find out more and create your personalised Noddy book!

www.MyNODDYBook.co.uk